MOG'S MISSING

by Helen Nicoll
and Jan Pieńkowski

PUFFIN BOOKS

It was
Midsummer
Eve

Meg was meeting
Bess, Jess, Tess and Cress

He wanted to go hunting

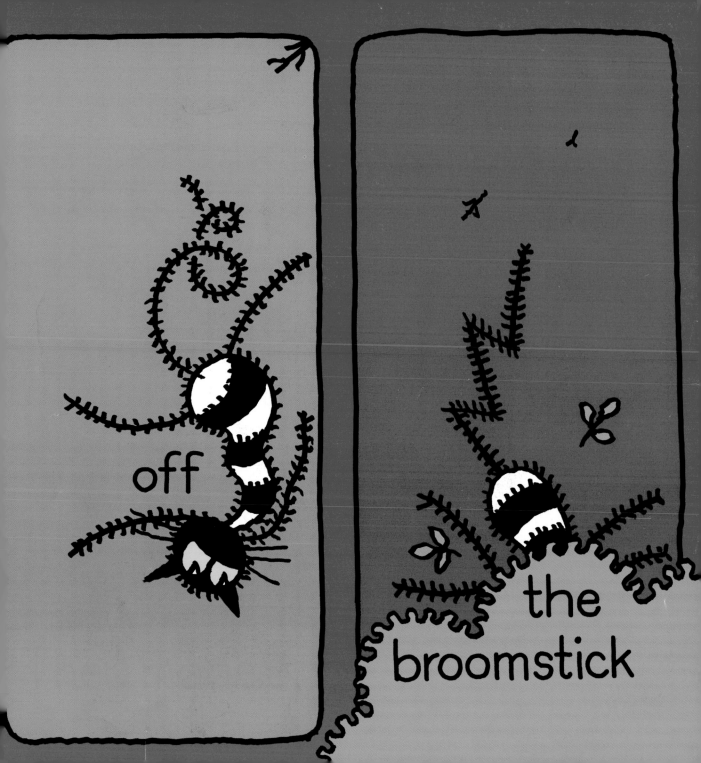

the
broomstick

into an ash tree

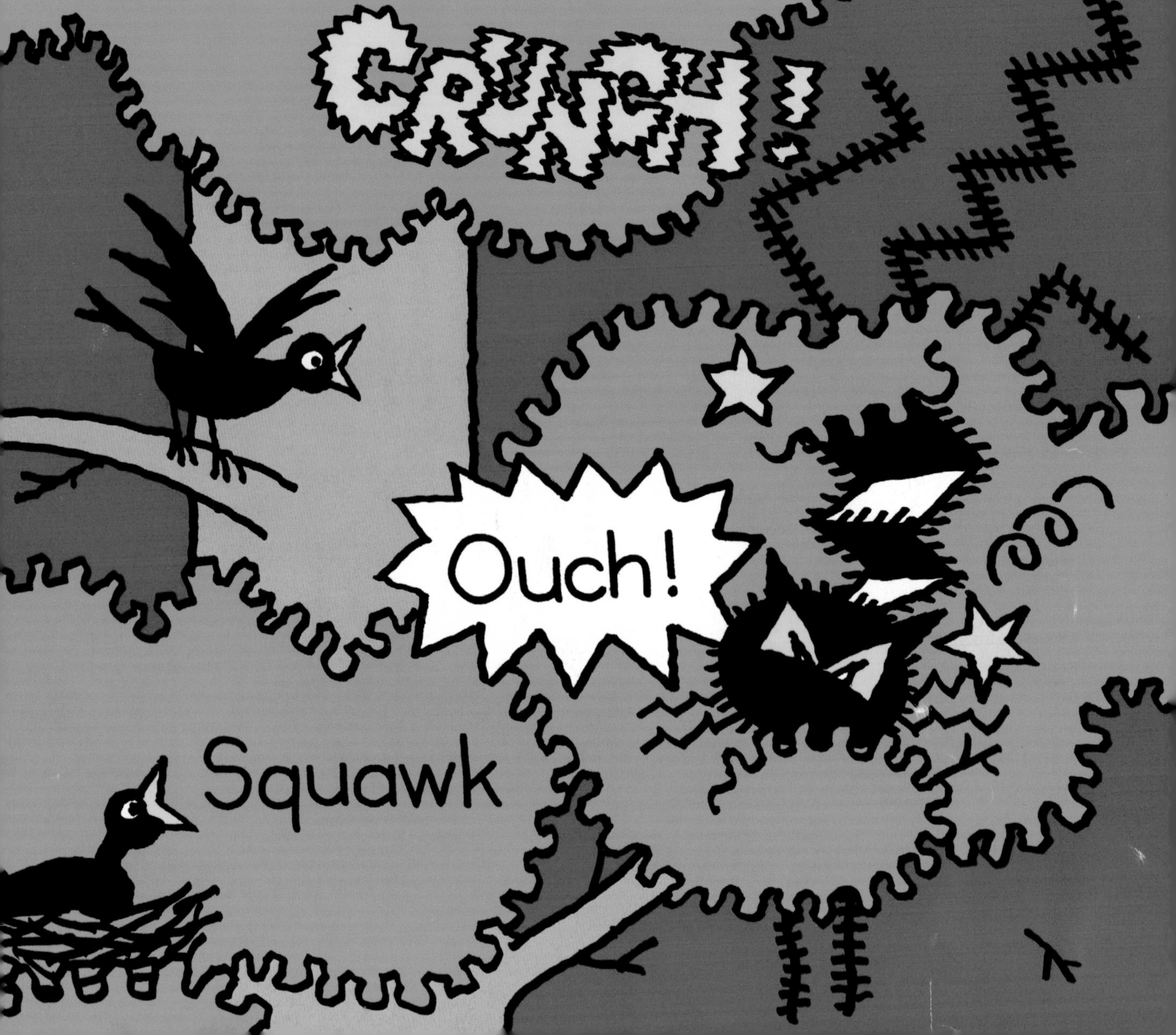

They met

CRASH!!

Mog was not up the ash tree

He was not in the hollow oak

He was not down a rabbit hole

They couldn't find him anywhere

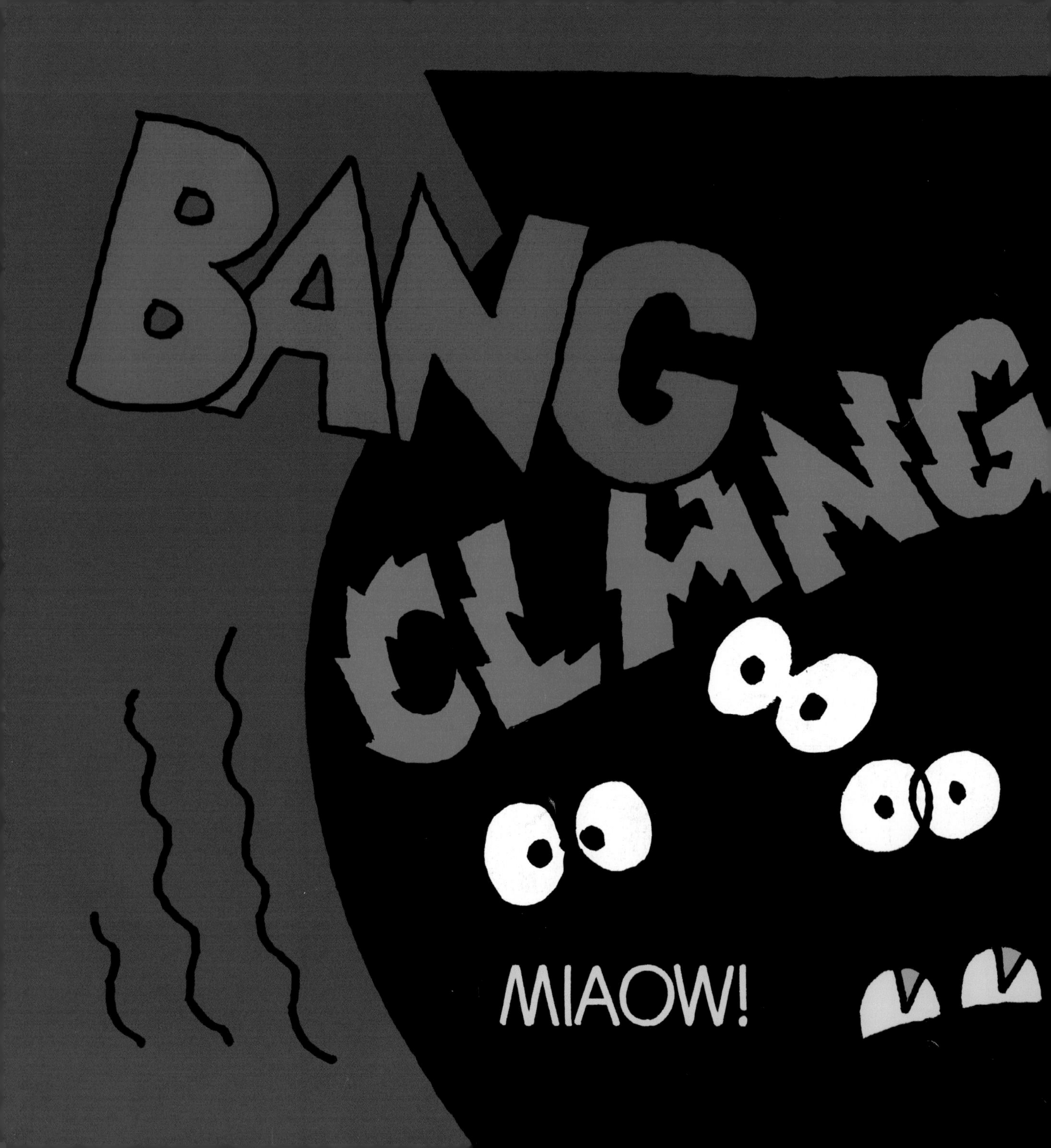
BANG
CLANG
MIAOW!

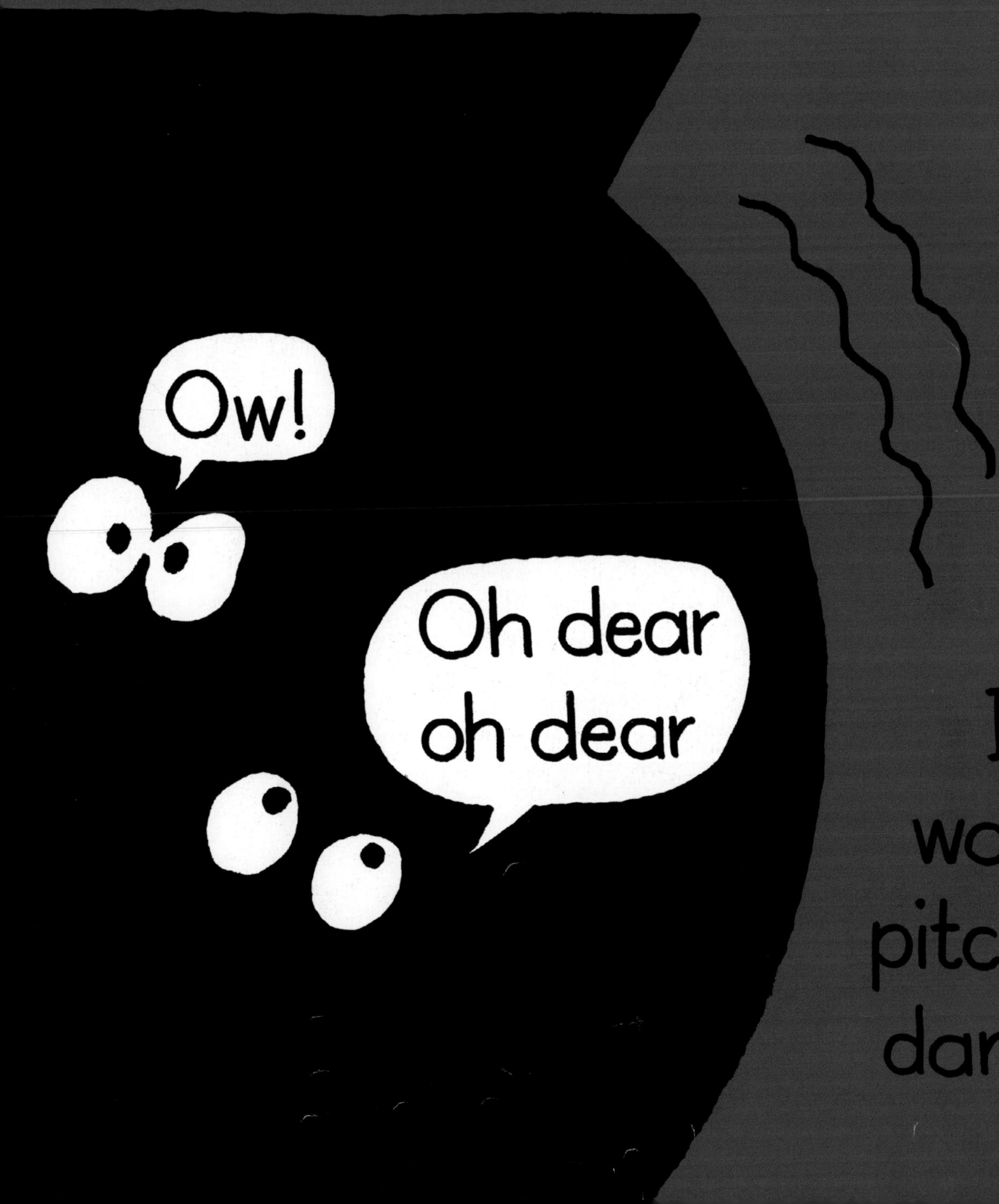

It was pitch dark

They were all in the cauldron

with Mog

Meg and Mog flew home

Goodbye!

for Yacine, Hédi and Sherif

PUFFIN BOOKS
Published by the Penguin Group. London, New York, Ireland, Australia, Canada, India, New Zealand and South Africa
Penguin Books Ltd. Registered Offices: 80 Strand, London WC2R 0RL, England
www.penguin.com
Published 2005
10 9 8 7 6 5 4 3 2 1
Text copyright © Helen Nicoll, 2005
Illustrations copyright © Jan Pieńkowski, 2005
Story and characters copyright © Helen Nicoll and Jan Pieńkowski, 2005
All rights reserved
The moral right of the author and illustrator has been asserted
Lettering by Caroline Austin
Manufactured in China
British Library Cataloguing in Publication Data
A CIP catalogue record for this book is available from the British Library
ISBN 0-141-38163-9